The Great Garbage Sale

Marilyn Helmer
Illustrated by Mike Deas

ORCA BOOK PUBLISHERS

For Sawyer and Levi,
who I'll bet will be great readers. —M.H.

Text copyright © 2013 Marilyn Helmer
Illustrations copyright © 2013 Mike Deas

Library and Archives Canada Cataloguing in Publication

Helmer, Marilyn
The great garage sale / Marilyn Helmer ; illustrated by Mike Deas.
(Orca echoes)

Issued also in electronic formats.
ISBN 978-1-4598-0060-1

I. Deas, Mike, 1982- II. Title. III. Series: Orca echoes

PS8565.E4594G74 2013   jc813'.54   C2012-907258-3

First published in the United States, 2013
Library of Congress Control Number: 2012952389

Summary: DJ mistakenly sells the wrong jewelry box to his friend at his
grandma's garage sale and has to sacrifice his beloved skateboard to make things right.

Orca Book Publishers gratefully acknowledges the support for its publishing programs
provided by the following agencies: the Government of Canada through the Canada Book Fund
and the Canada Council for the Arts, and the Province of British Columbia
through the BC Arts Council and the Book Publishing Tax Credit.

MIX
Paper from
responsible sources
FSC® C004071

ANCIENT FOREST ™
FRIENDLY

*Orca Book Publishers is dedicated to preserving the environment and has printed
this book on Forest Stewardship Council® certified paper.*

Cover artwork and interior illustrations by Mike Deas
Author photo by Gary Helmer

ORCA BOOK PUBLISHERS
PO BOX 5626, STN. B
VICTORIA, BC CANADA
V8R 6S4

ORCA BOOK PUBLISHERS
PO BOX 468
CUSTER, WA USA
98240-0468

www.orcabook.com
Printed and bound in Canada.

16 15 14 13 • 4 3 2 1

CHAPTER ONE
Disasters

"Thirty-one, thirty-two..." DJ yanked another weed from the garden and tossed it into the bucket. Wait till Mom found out he had weeded the garden, all by himself, without even being asked. Wouldn't she be surprised!

Yank, toss. Yank, toss. Maybe Mom would be so happy about the weeding, she would forget about the peanut-butter disaster this morning. The memory played through DJ's mind like a bad movie.

They were dog-sitting Rufus Crudley. Rufus was Uncle Dave's dog. He was the best dog in the world, except for one thing. Rufus would eat anything he could get his jaws around. That is how the disaster happened.

DJ had made himself a Super Stacker for lunch. Salami, two kinds of cheese, onion, sun-dried tomatoes, raisins and peanut butter. He took it into the den and sat on the sofa. Oops—he'd forgotten the milk. He put his Super Stacker down and went to the kitchen.

Unfortunately, DJ had also forgotten two strict rules. One—never leave food on the sofa. Two—never, ever leave food alone when Rufus Crudley is around.

DJ heard a choking, gagging sound. He raced back to the den. Fortunately, the piece Rufus was choking on came up. Unfortunately, so did the rest of the Super Stacker. All over Mom's brand-new sofa.

As he yanked out another weed, a voice broke into his thoughts. "What are you doing?"

DJ looked over his shoulder. A kid he had never seen before stood behind him.

The kid was dressed in ripped jeans and a too-large T-shirt. The T-shirt was a riot of wild colors.

On his feet was a pair of red high-top joggers. A large cowboy hat sat low on his head.

Fan-tabulous! DJ was impressed. If only his mom would let him dress like that.

"What are you doing?" the kid repeated. His voice was low and husky.

DJ swiped a dirt-streaked hand across his face. "I'm weeding my mom's garden. I'm going to surprise her."

"She's going to be surprised, all right," said the kid. "You're pulling out flowers, not weeds." His mouth curved into a lopsided grin. "Don't you know the difference between a weed and a flower?"

"Of course I do," said DJ. Who was this smart-alecky kid anyway? "Weeds don't have flowers on them."

The kid rolled his eyes. "See those buds? You're pulling out plants before they're big enough to bloom."

DJ looked into the bucket. Panic! Most of the plants had buds on them, but they were so tiny you could hardly see them.

"You want some advice?" asked the kid. "Replant them. Pronto. Maybe they'll still grow." He picked up the bucket and sorted through the contents. "You have a couple of weeds, but the rest are flowers." He dropped the flowers at DJ's feet and dumped the weeds back into the bucket.

DJ began replanting, scattering dirt in all directions.

The kid watched for a few minutes. "Water them when you're finished," he said. "I've got to go." He headed down the street.

DJ pulled off his cap and fanned his face. His curly red hair stuck out in all directions. "Hey," he called. "My name's DJ. What's yours?"

The kid turned and snatched off the cowboy hat. Long dark curls spilled out. The kid grinned a lopsided grin. "My name's Samantha," she called back. "But call me Sam. See ya."

She ran on down the street, leaving DJ staring in wide-eyed astonishment.

CHAPTER TWO
Garage Sale

On Saturday morning, DJ checked the garden. He had checked it every day that week. The replanted plants were growing. That girl Sam was right. Since yesterday, two had bloomed. Fan-tabulous!

Mom came up behind him. "You did a great job weeding." She gave DJ a suspicious look. "Why this sudden interest in gardening?"

DJ shrugged. He hadn't told his mom about the weeding disaster. He had fixed it, thanks to Sam's advice. Sometimes it was best not to talk about fixed disasters.

"Grandma phoned," said Mom. "She wants to know when you're coming to help with her garage sale."

"I forgot." DJ shot to his feet. "I said I'd be there at nine o'clock."

Mom glanced at her watch. "You're two hours late."

DJ charged across the garden.

"David Jeremiah!" Mom clamped her hands to her head. "Look where you're going. You almost stepped on my prize rosebush."

"Sorry, Mom." DJ dashed toward the house. "If I broke anything, I'll fix it when I get home."

"Change your clothes," Mom called after him. "Wash your hands."

DJ raced to the bathroom. He rinsed his hands under the tap. The water turned brown. DJ reached for a towel. Oops—better not. Mom's favorite rosebud ones were hanging neatly on the rack. He dried his hands on his jeans instead.

In his room, DJ changed into clean shorts and his favorite T-shirt. A happy-faced monkey skateboarded across the front. He noticed a lump in the middle of the bed. He put his hand under the quilt and pulled out a little gray sock monkey.

DJ looked over his shoulder. No one was watching. He gave the sock monkey a hug and propped him on his pillow. "Bye, Sockster," he said. "I have to go. Grandma needs me to run her garage sale."

DJ hurried to the kitchen. There wasn't time to make a Super Stacker. Super Stackers were DJ's favorite food. No one could make a Super Stacker like he could.

He stuffed a banana into his pocket. That would keep him going until he had time to make another Super Stacker.

DJ jammed his helmet on his head. He grabbed his skateboard and ran outside. "Go, Speedwell!" he shouted, and he zipped down the street.

CHAPTER THREE
Sam Again

As DJ whipped around the corner, he almost collided with Sam.

"Hi ya," said Sam. Today she was wearing an orange and green shirt. Her ripped jeans were splattered with bright yellow paint. She had a black marker in one hand.

"Hi," said DJ. "What are you doing?"

Sam jerked a thumb at the sign on a post. "I'm fixing the sign. Whoever made it can't spell."

DJ looked at the sign.

Great Garbage Sale today!

9 a.m.–1 p.m.

Super Stuff

Really Cheep
123 Birdwhistle Drive
All Sales Final!

DJ had made that sign himself, and he was proud of it. Sam had drawn a black X through the *b* in *Garage*. She had changed the second *e* in *CHEEP* to an *a*.

DJ frowned. "You messed up my sign."

"Your sign?" Sam rolled her eyes. "You should thank me. I fixed it for you. You don't know how to spell. There's no *b* in *garage*. And c-h-e-e-p is the sound a bird makes."

DJ huffed a sigh. He was good at everything in school except spelling. How could anyone keep twenty-six letters in the right order in all those gazillions of words?

"Where is the garage sale?" asked Sam.

"It's up the street at my grandma's house," said DJ. "Do you want to come?"

"Maybe," said Sam. She looked at DJ's skateboard. "That's a neat skateboard. Is it for sale?"

DJ's eyes almost popped out of his head. "Speedwell? For sale? No. Never. Not ever."

"Speedwell?" Sam grinned. "You gave your skateboard a name?"

"Why not?" said DJ. He gave all his favorite things a name.

"I wish I had a skateboard," said Sam.

"Come to the garage sale," said DJ. "My grandma has lots of great stuff."

"Does she have a skateboard?" asked Sam.

DJ shook his head. "She just skis and snowboards."

Sam looked at the sign. "The garage sale ends at one PM, right? That's when I'll come. That's when stuff is really c-h-e-a-p."

DJ pretended he didn't hear the spelling. "Do you live around here?"

Sam nodded. "I live two blocks over, on Huckleberry Lane. We just moved in."

"I'd better go," said DJ. "I'll see you later."

Sam shrugged. "Maybe."

13

CHAPTER FOUR
Tiger the Terrible

The garage sale was busy. DJ put Speedwell on the porch, safely under a big lounge chair.

Grandma hurried over. "DJ, where have you been?" She ran a hand through her hair. It was as red and curly as DJ's. Today she was dressed from head to toe in purple and turquoise. Even her sunglasses had purple frames with turquoise sparkles. DJ thought Grandma was one cool dresser.

Before DJ could say a word, Grandma hurried on. "Sweetie, I need you to do me a favor." She handed him a key. "Rita Rowbottom asked me to sell a box of her costume jewelry. I forgot about it until now. Would you run over and get it, please?"

DJ gulped. Ms. Rowbottom lived in the big house next door. She was very friendly. But Ms. Rowbottom was not the only one who lived in that house. Tiger the Terrible lived there too.

Tiger was a humongous orange, black-and-white striped cat. She was anything but friendly. The mailman had nicknamed her Tiger the Terrible. DJ thought it was the perfect name for her. He was sure Tiger really was a tiger.

Whenever Tiger saw DJ, she yowled and growled and hissed. She had very sharp claws. DJ had found that out the first time he rushed over to pat her.

"Grandma, I don't think—" DJ began.

A man came over with an armload of books. "How much for the lot?" he asked.

"Rita said she would leave the box on the kitchen table," Grandma said to DJ. She turned to the man and they began to bargain.

DJ sighed. Grandma was depending on him. How much damage could one cat do? He remembered the scratches. Ouch! A lot.

DJ walked slowly across the driveway and up the steps to Ms. Rowbottom's front door. He took a deep breath, squared his shoulders and prepared to face Tiger the Terrible. He hoped he would come back alive.

CHAPTER FIVE
Facing the Tiger

DJ opened the door. The house was silent. Tiger the Terrible was nowhere to be seen. DJ breathed a huge sigh of relief and raced toward the kitchen. Then he heard it—a terrible yowling, growling, tiger-in-the-jungle sound.

DJ skidded to a stop. Tiger the Terrible guarded the kitchen doorway. Her tail stood up like a bristle brush. Her fur puffed out like a dust mop. She looked three sizes bigger than usual.

DJ took a step closer. Tiger the Terrible hissed like a deflating bicycle tire.

Thoughts whirled through DJ's head. He had to

get past Tiger the Terrible. He had to get that box of jewelry. But how?

Wait. Karate! Of course, he would never hurt Tiger the Terrible. He would just demonstrate a few of his karate chops. That would show her who was boss.

DJ flailed his arms wildly. Tiger the Terrible wasn't impressed. She swatted at his leg with bared claws.

DJ jumped back. He bumped against the hall table. A small box slid onto the floor. Clunky, chunky necklaces spilled out.

DJ let out a whoop that sent Tiger the Terrible scrambling under a chair. Ms. Rowbottom had left her jewelry box on the hall table. He didn't have to get past Tiger the Terrible after all.

DJ grabbed the box and raced back up the hall. He closed the door firmly behind him. No way was Tiger the Terrible going to get out and scare away Grandma's customers.

Grandma saw DJ racing toward her. "You're a lifesaver," she said as he handed her the jewelry box.

"I almost needed my life saved," said DJ. "I was attacked trying to get that box."

"Attacked?" Grandma gasped. "Who on earth—?"

"Tiger the Terrible," said DJ. "She was guarding the doorway. She wouldn't let me past."

Grandma shook her head. "DJ, that sweet little cat wouldn't hurt a flea."

"Sweet! Little! Cat!" said DJ. "Grandma, Tiger the Terrible could wipe out a whole army of fleas."

Grandma wasn't listening. She turned the jewelry box over. "The price sticker must have fallen off. No matter. Rita told me she wants five dollars for it." Grandma wrote *$5.00* on a piece of tape and stuck it on the box. "Let's hope someone buys it."

Who would buy a box of clunky, chunky necklaces? DJ wondered. But he kept that thought to himself.

CHAPTER SIX
Super Stacker

Customers buzzed around the tables like bees in a hive. DJ was so busy, he hardly had time to think.

"Hey, dude," a voice called out. "How much do you want for this?"

DJ turned. A boy with purple hair, two nose rings and a tattoo of a gecko on one cheek stood behind him. He was holding Speedwell.

"What are you doing with my skateboard?" DJ gasped. He glanced at the porch. The big lounge chair he had hidden Speedwell under was gone. Grandma must have sold it.

"So—how much do you want for the skateboard?" the boy asked impatiently.

"Speedwell is not for sale." DJ said each word like it was a separate sentence.

"Speedwell?" The boy snickered. "You gave your skateboard a name?"

"Why not?" DJ frowned. Sam had asked that too. What was so funny about giving your special things a name?

The boy handed Speedwell back to DJ. "You are one weird dude," he said.

DJ raced up the steps and into the house. He put Speedwell in the hall closet and shut the door. No one else was going to get their hands on his Speedwell.

An hour passed. Fewer people came by.

"It will soon be time to close up," said Grandma. She sniffed. "DJ, you smell like a banana."

DJ sniffed. He did smell like a banana. He shoved his hand into his pocket. Yuck! Squishy, linty banana stuck to his fingers. "I was so busy I forgot about my snack," he said.

"You had better clean that mess out of your pocket," said Grandma. "While you're at it, make yourself something to eat."

DJ didn't wait for a second invitation.

"Help yourself to anything in the fridge," Grandma called after him.

"Fan-tabulous!" DJ cheered. "Super Stacker, here I come." The front door slammed behind him.

DJ cleaned the mess out of his pocket. He still smelled like a banana, but he didn't mind. The smell went with his monkey T-shirt.

DJ opened the fridge. Inside was a Super Stacker sandwich maker's dream. Leftover tuna, provolone, avocado dip, pepper jelly, pineapple and something curly that looked like lettuce. Fan-tabulous! He got peanut butter and bread from the cupboard and set to work.

DJ built his Super Stacker in layers. It was like building a house. You had to work carefully so it didn't collapse. Peanut butter was the cement that held everything together. DJ poured himself a big glass of milk. He ate every single bite of his masterpiece. No one, absolutely no one, could make a Super Stacker like he could.

CHAPTER SEVEN
One More Sale

"We haven't had any customers since you went in for lunch," Grandma said when DJ came back outside. "Can I leave you in charge while I make a cup of tea?"

"No problem-o, Grandma," said DJ. DJ loved to be left in charge.

Minutes passed. No one else came by. Being in charge was no fun if there was nothing to be in charge of.

DJ got Speedwell from the closet. He zipped up and down the street. He spun around and did a wheelie. That's when he saw Sam. She was looking through Ms. Rowbottom's jewelry box.

Sam had a pink bag with green cats on it slung over her shoulder. She was still wearing her paint-splattered jeans. Now her T-shirt was splattered with yellow paint too.

"Hi ya," she said when she saw DJ. She sniffed as he came closer. "Are you wearing perfume? You smell like a banana."

"I am not wearing perfume!" DJ told her. He explained about the squished banana.

"I like bananas too," said Sam. "But I don't want to smell like one." She held up the jewelry box. "I'll give you two dollars for it."

"Two dollars?" DJ shook his head. "No way. It's marked five dollars."

"Garage sales are for bargaining," said Sam.

"I can't," said DJ. "I'm selling it for Ms. Rowbottom. She wants five dollars for it."

Sam picked out a couple of necklaces and put them on. "What do you think?"

DJ thought they were the ugliest necklaces he had ever seen, but he didn't want to hurt Sam's feelings. "They look really funny on you," he said.

Sam rolled her eyes. She reached into her bag and took out an envelope marked *Happy Birthday, Samantha*. She pulled a five-dollar bill from the envelope and handed it to DJ. Then she scooped up the jewelry box and put it into her bag. "I'm helping my dad paint our garage door. See ya." She ran down the street with the bag swinging on her shoulder.

DJ was impressed. Sam ran almost as fast as he could move on Speedwell.

CHAPTER EIGHT
Another Disaster

The garage sale was over. Grandma started packing up the leftovers.

"I'll get the sign," said DJ. "We can save it for next year."

When DJ came back, Ms. Rowbottom's car was parked in her driveway.

"Rita's home," said Grandma. "She'll be over as soon as she feeds Tiger."

DJ wondered what Ms. Rowbottom fed Tiger the Terrible. He hoped it wasn't anything that was alive.

Moments later, Ms. Rowbottom came hurrying across the driveway. She had a box in her hand. "You forgot my jewelry," she said.

31

Grandma looked at her in surprise. "Rita, we did get your jewelry."

Ms. Rowbottom shook her head. "When I came home, the box was still on the kitchen table where I left it."

"But I found the jewelry box on the hall table," said DJ.

Ms. Rowbottom let out a piercing shriek. Her eyes were two jack-o'-lantern Os of shock. "DJ, please tell me you did not sell the box of jewelry I left on the hall table."

DJ gulped. The leftover tuna, provolone, avocado dip, pepper jelly, pineapple, something curly that looked like lettuce, and peanut butter Super Stacker churned in his stomach. "Yes, I did," he said in a not-another-disaster voice.

"Didn't you see the box on the kitchen table?" asked Ms. Rowbottom.

"I...I didn't go into the kitchen." DJ swallowed. "I saw the box on the hall table. I thought you had

left it there instead." He got the five-dollar bill from the money box to hand to Ms. Rowbottom.

Ms. Rowbottom scarcely glanced at the bill. "This is a disaster! A horrible disaster!" she cried. "My favorite necklaces were in that box."

Grandma clapped her hands to her cheeks. "Rita, I am so sorry. I feel terrible about this."

"A disaster! A horrible disaster!" Ms. Rowbottom moaned. "How could this have happened?"

"I am so sorry," Grandma repeated. "It's all my fault."

DJ felt sick with misery. It wasn't Grandma's fault. It was his fault.

Grandma turned to him. "DJ, do you remember who bought that box?"

"Yes, I do!" DJ breathed a huge sigh of relief. "It was that girl, Sam."

"Do you know where she lives?" asked Grandma.

"Not exactly," said DJ, "but I'll find her." He stuffed the five-dollar bill into his pocket and hopped

34

onto Speedwell. "Don't worry, Ms. Rowbottom," he called over his shoulder. "I'll get your jewelry back no matter what."

CHAPTER NINE
A Clue

DJ sped toward Huckleberry Lane. All I have to do is find Sam, he told himself. I'll explain what happened. I will give her money back. She will give Ms. Rowbottom's jewelry back. No problem-o.

As DJ turned onto Huckleberry Lane, a horrible thought struck him. Problem-o. Major problem-o! He had no idea which house was Sam's.

Huckleberry Lane was a short street, but even a short street has lots of houses. How could he find Sam's house? There was only one way. He would have to knock on every door until he found her.

DJ walked up to the first house. A man answered the door.

"Does Sam live here?" DJ asked.

The man shook his head. "Not anymore."

Not anymore? "Where did she go?" DJ asked.

"She?" The man looked at DJ. "My son Sam is a *he*. And *he* is away at university."

"Your Sam isn't the Sam I'm looking for," said DJ.

"Good luck finding her," said the man as he closed the door.

To DJ's surprise, Sam was a popular name on Huckleberry Lane. He asked a woman working in her garden if she knew where Sam lived.

"Next door," said the woman, "in the backyard."

"Sam lives in the backyard?" DJ gasped.

The woman pointed. "There's Sam now."

DJ followed her finger. Standing at the fence was the biggest dog DJ had ever seen. The dog barked. It sounded like rumbling thunder.

"Don't be afraid of him," said the woman. "He's a big old pussycat. He's very friendly."

DJ thought of Tiger the Terrible. "Big old pussycats aren't always friendly," he said.

Next, DJ asked a teenager walking his dog. "Sorry, kid," said the teenager. "I don't have a clue where Sam lives."

"A *clue* where Sam lives…" The words blared through DJ's head. He looked up and down the street. Then he saw it.

The teenager didn't have a clue where Sam lived, but DJ did. In fact, he knew exactly where Sam lived. He took off down the street.

CHAPTER TEN
All Sales Final

When Sam came to Grandma's garage sale, she had been wearing jeans splattered with yellow paint. She had said she was helping her dad paint their garage door. The house DJ was standing in front of had a yellow garage door. Above it was a *Wet Paint* sign.

DJ raced up the steps and rang the bell.

A woman opened the door. She had dark springy curls all over her head, like Sam. She was wearing a jumble-of-colors T-shirt, like Sam's.

DJ held back an earsplitting whoop. "Does Sam live here?" he asked.

"Yes, she does," said the woman. "Samantha!" she called into the house.

Sam came to the door. She had three clunky, chunky necklaces around her neck. She looked at DJ in surprise. "How did you know where I live?"

"Easy peasy detective work," said DJ. He told Sam about the yellow-paint clue. Then he told her about the jewelry-box mix-up. "So I have to get the jewelry back," he said.

"No way," said Sam. "Your sign said *All sales final.*"

DJ shifted Speedwell from one hand to the other. He took Sam's five-dollar bill from his pocket. "Please, Sam," he said. "I have to get Ms. Rowbottom's jewelry back."

Sam shrugged. "Sorry. All sales final."

DJ was desperate. "I'll do anything to get that jewelry back."

A lopsided grin spread across Sam's face. "How about a trade?"

"Fan-tabulous," said DJ. "What do you want to trade?"

Sam pointed to Speedwell.

41

DJ's jaw dropped in disbelief. "I can't trade Speedwell," he said. "No way. No how."

Sam shrugged again. "It's up to you. If you really want the jewelry back, you'll have to give me your skateboard."

Ms. Rowbottom's words flashed across DJ's mind. "A horrible disaster." That's exactly what this was. Grandma thought it was her fault. But it was his fault. He was the one who had taken the wrong box.

DJ had no choice. A promise was a promise. With a sinking heart, he handed Speedwell to Sam.

CHAPTER ELEVEN
Speedwell

"My hero!" Ms. Rowbottom shrieked when DJ returned with her jewelry box. She hugged DJ so hard, she knocked off his helmet. Ms. Rowbottom was too excited to notice.

DJ picked up his helmet. A golf ball-sized lump formed in his throat. Without Speedwell, he wouldn't need his helmet anymore. Next summer he would probably sell it at Grandma's garage sale.

When he got home, DJ went to his room. He put Sam's five dollars into his monkey bank.

In bed that night, he told Sockster what had happened. "This was the worst, most tragic day of my whole life," he said. "It was a horrible, terrible disaster." DJ and Sockster tossed and turned until late into the night.

The next morning, DJ trudged into the kitchen. "Good morning, Mom," he said in a quiet indoor voice. He sat at the table and propped his chin on his hands.

Mom was surprised. DJ never walked into a room. He ran. He never sat in a chair. He straddled it, pretending it was a wild bronco. And he hardly ever spoke in an indoor voice.

"What kind of cereal would you like?" Mom asked.

DJ sighed so hard, he blew a couple of leaves off Mom's plant. "I may never eat again," he said.

Mom poured some Crispy Crunchies into a bowl. She sliced a banana on top and put it in front of DJ.

DJ forced himself to eat, one small spoonful at a time.

"Your friend Riley will be back next week," Mom said to cheer him up. "Then you'll have someone to skateboard with."

DJ dropped the spoon halfway to his mouth. He slumped so low, he almost slid out of his chair. He hadn't told Mom about Speedwell yet. Now was as bad a time as any.

"Mom…" DJ began.

The phone rang. Then the doorbell chimed.

Mom reached for the phone.

DJ dragged himself to the door.

Sam stood on the porch. She had on a bright orange helmet with a happy face. Sam's face was anything but happy. Under one arm was Speedwell.

CHAPTER TWELVE
Ah-mazing!

"What are you doing here?" asked DJ. "How did you know where I live?"

"Easy peasy detective work," said Sam. "Your name and phone number are on the bottom of your skateboard. And speaking of your skateboard, you can have it back." She shoved Speedwell into DJ's arms.

DJ was too stunned to speak.

"I want my five dollars back," said Sam.

DJ found his voice. "Wait right here. Don't move. Don't breathe. I'll be back. Pronto."

DJ raced past the kitchen, up the stairs and into his room. He grabbed his monkey bank and dug out Sam's money. He snatched up his helmet and charged downstairs, whooping like a cheerleader for a winning team.

Mom looked out of the kitchen. "Is everything okay?"

DJ stopped long enough to give her a high five. "Everything isn't okay, Mom. It's fan-tabulous!" he said as he ran out the door.

Sam put the money into her pocket. "There's something wrong with your skateboard," she said.

"What are you talking about?" said DJ. "Speedwell is the best skateboard in the whole world."

"I keep falling off," said Sam.

DJ put Speedwell on the ground. He zipped up and down the driveway. He did wheelies. He jumped off, flipped Speedwell and caught it in one hand. "Speedwell works perfectly," he said. "No problem-o."

"You are ah-mazing," said Sam. She grinned her lopsided grin. "I wish I could skateboard like that."

DJ grinned too. No one had ever called him *ah-mazing* before. "I could teach you how," he said.

"Would you?" asked Sam

"No problem-o," said DJ.

For the next hour, Sam and DJ took turns on Speedwell.

Sam learned quickly. "I love skateboarding," she said, zipping along like a pro. She still couldn't do wheelies though.

DJ showed her again. He loved teaching people how to do things.

"I need more practice," said Sam. "It's lunchtime. I have to go home. Can we skateboard tomorrow?"

"Sure," said DJ. Teaching Sam to skateboard was fun. Having someone to skateboard with, especially someone who thought he was ah-mazing, was even more fun.

"Come over to my house tomorrow morning," said Sam. She took off running.

DJ watched. That Sam was one fast runner. Maybe he would challenge her to a race tomorrow. He watched as she flew down the street. Or maybe not.

CHAPTER THIRTEEN
Sam's House

DJ raced into the kitchen. He made a peanut butter, banana, kiwi, blueberry, honey and yogurt Super Stacker. Had he missed anything? Yes, liverwurst. He heaped some on.

He was finishing the last delicious bite when the phone rang.

"DJ, it's Sam…something ah-mazing…you're not going to believe it." Sam's words tumbled over one another.

"What happened?" asked DJ.

"You'll see when you get here. Hurry up." Sam hung up without saying goodbye.

Something ah-mazing? Fan-tabulous! DJ went to the den to tell his mom where he was going.

Mom looked up from her computer. "Have fun," she said. "Remember you have to clean the garage this afternoon."

DJ groaned. He had forgotten. He often forgot chores like that. "Can I do it tomorrow?" he asked.

"No way," said Mom in her not-budging voice. "I want it cleaned this afternoon for sure."

DJ sighed. "I'll remember," he promised.

He grabbed Speedwell and headed for Sam's.

When he turned onto Huckleberry Lane, he stopped in surprise. Sam was coming to meet him—on a skateboard.

"Guess what?" said Sam. "My cousin got a new skateboard for his birthday. He sold me his old one." She gave DJ a high five. "Let's race," she said and zipped off.

DJ and Sam skateboarded for the rest of the morning. When they went in for a drink, Sam's mom invited DJ to stay for lunch.

DJ loved eating at other people's houses. He called his mom.

"You can stay, but you'll have to come right home afterward," said Mom.

"Why?" asked DJ.

Mom sighed. "You have to clean the garage. Remember? It needs to be done this afternoon for sure. Oh, and remember to say thank you and be polite."

"Okay," DJ promised. How was he supposed to remember all that stuff?

"Do you want to see my room?" Sam asked when he hung up. "I decorated it myself."

DJ shrugged. Bedrooms were boring. Then he remembered what Mom had said about being polite. "Sure, okay, great," he said. "I love looking at bedrooms." Mom would have been proud of him.

CHAPTER FOURTEEN
Super Stackers and Roll-ups

DJ followed Sam down the hall. He stopped in the doorway. He had never seen a bedroom like Sam's before. It was like stepping into a giant paint box.

The walls were purple. The carpet was bright green. A rainbow-colored quilt covered the bed. In one corner, a huge orange bear sat on a yellow chair beside a pink dresser.

"My dad says I have a wild imagination," said Sam.

"My dad says the same about me," said DJ. Actually, a lot of people said DJ had a wild imagination. DJ didn't mind. People with wild imaginations were his favorite kind.

DJ noticed a picture on Sam's dresser. It was a photo of a large black-and-white cat. The cat had a scowly face. It reminded DJ of Tiger the Terrible.

"That was my cat Hairball," said Sam. "He was kind of grumpy."

DJ told Sam about Tiger the Terrible and the jewelry box.

"Were you afraid of her?" Sam asked.

"Well…" DJ hesitated.

"Don't feel bad," said Sam. "Everyone on our street was afraid of Hairball."

DJ grinned. Sam understood.

"I'm hungry," said Sam. "Let's have lunch."

Sam's mom was in the kitchen making coffee.

"Can we make our own sandwiches?" Sam asked.

"Okay," said Sam's mom. "But maybe DJ would prefer a plain sandwich rather than one of your quirky creations."

DJ's stomach growled. A quirky-creation sandwich sounded interesting and delicious.

"I'll get back to unpacking," said Sam's mom. She smiled at DJ. "Good luck."

Sam opened the fridge door. She took out a container marked *Spicy Chicken*. She took out salsa, two kinds of cheese, half a sausage, a raw onion, grainy mustard and chickpeas. She took out tortilla wraps. "I'm going to make Roll-Ups," she said.

"What are Roll-Ups?" asked DJ.

"You'll see," said Sam.

DJ watched Sam spread mustard on the tortilla wraps. He smacked his lips as she layered on chicken, cheese, sausage, onion and chickpeas. His mouth watered as she put neat dabs of salsa on top.

Sam rolled up the wraps and handed one to DJ.

DJ took a bite. He took another bite. "Fan-tabulous," he said. "Ah-mazingly fan-tabulous."

Sam took a bite of hers. "Fan-tabulously ah-mazing," she said.

When they finished eating, Sam said, "I have a new computer game. Do you want to play?"

"I can't," DJ said reluctantly. "I have to clean the garage this afternoon for sure."

Sam laughed. "That sounds like something my mom would say. Do you want some help?"

DJ stared at Sam. She was offering to help him clean the garage? "For real?" he asked.

"Are there any spiders in your garage?" Sam asked.

Uh-oh. Was Sam afraid of spiders? "Well, sometimes," said DJ.

"Fan-tabulous," said Sam. "Spiders are cool."

DJ grinned. "They're ah-mazing."

They went to the den to tell Sam's mom. DJ remembered to thank her for inviting him to stay for lunch.

Sam's mom smiled. "So you survived one of Sam's quirky creations," she said.

"Sam makes the best quirky-creation Roll-Ups in the world," said DJ. He turned to Sam. "Tomorrow you can come to my house for lunch. I'll make you a peanut butter, banana, stinky cheese, walnut and tortilla chip Super Stacker."

"What's a Super Stacker?" asked Sam.

"You'll see," said DJ.

Marilyn Helmer was born in St. John's, Newfoundland, grew up in Montreal and now lives with her husband near Belwood, Ontario. She is the author of many children's books, including picture books, early readers, novels, riddle books and retold tales. *The Great Garage Sale* is Marilyn's fifth book with Orca Book Publishers and her fourth in the Orca Echoes series. For more information, visit www.marilynhelmer.com.